SCOOBY-DOO! PICTURE CLUE BOOK

THE HAUNTED PUMPKINS

By Michelle H. Nagler
Illustrated by Duendes del Sur

Hello Reader — Level 1

No part of this publication may be reproduced in whole or in part,
or stored in a retrieval system, or transmitted in any form or by any means,
electronic, mechanical, photocopying, recording, or otherwise, without written
permission of the publisher. For information regarding permission, write to Scholastic Inc.,
Attention: Permissions Department, 555 Broadway, New York, NY 10012.

ISBN 0-439-31836-X

Designed by Maria Stasavage

Printed in the U.S.A.

First Scholastic printing, September 2001

SCHOLASTIC INC.

New York Toronto London Auckland Sydney
Mexico City New Delhi Hong Kong Buenos Aires

 and his friends were making

a haunted 🏚 for Halloween.

They hung 🕸 on the 🪟.

They carved scary faces on 🎃.

was scared of the 🎃.

played a 📼 of scary sounds.

The 📼 said *"Woo-oooh!"* and

"Creeeeeak!" and *"Boo!"*

A line of people waited to see

the haunted .

and took their and

put them in a .

One little girl, Amy, was scared.

She didn't like the or the .

said, "It is just make-believe."

"I am not a real ," said .

But doesn't like the

either, Amy thought.

The next day, the 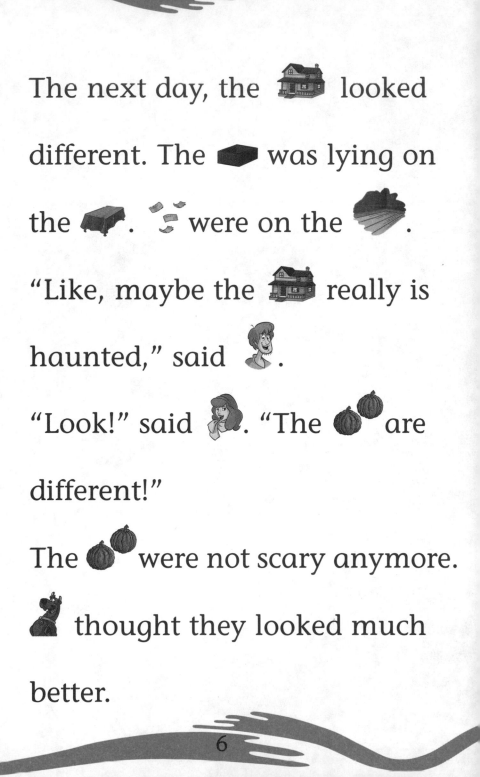 looked

different. The was lying on

the . were on the .

"Like, maybe the really is

haunted," said .

"Look!" said . "The are

different!"

The were not scary anymore.

 thought they looked much

better.

"Jinkies!" said . "Haunted !"

"Let's look for clues," said . ", , and I will look outside. , you and  look inside."

"Ro way!" said .

"The  is haunted!" said .

"Would you do it for two ?"  asked.

"Rokay!" said .

and heard a noise.

But it was just a scratching the .

"Look!" yelled , "a !"

But it was only a creepy shadow on the .

said, "Like, let's search the kitchen, ."

used his to find the way down the to the kitchen.

 and did not find any

clues in the kitchen.

But they did find a on

the .

As they were eating the ,

they heard scary noises.

"Zoinks!" said. "It's the !"

ran back up the and

out the .

 and were looking in the for clues.

"We heard the !" yelled .

"Reah!" said , running out the .

slipped on some on the and fell down the .

"Are you OK, ?" asked.

"Look!"  said, " found !"

 had landed on a pile of  near some .

"And a trail of  too!" said .

"Let's follow them," said .

"Yeah,"  said. "Let's get away from the  in the !"

"That was no , ,"  said. "I was just testing the  of scary noises."

The gang followed the  and
.

The trail went around the .

It went around a .

The  and  stopped at a

bunch of smelly .

"Yuck!" said .

 held his .

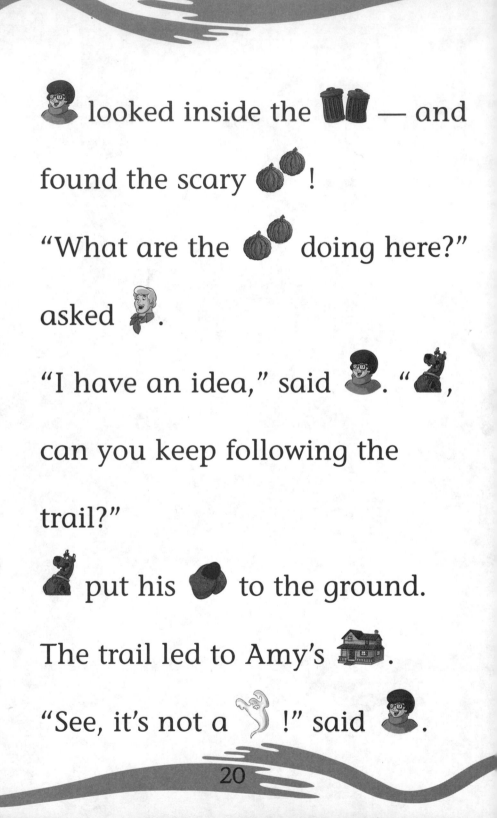

looked inside the 🗑️🗑️ — and found the scary 🎃🎃!

"What are the 🎃🎃 doing here?" asked 👦.

"I have an idea," said 👧. "🐕, can you keep following the trail?"

🐕 put his 👃 to the ground.

The trail led to Amy's 🏠.

"See, it's not a 👻 !" said 👧.

Amy said, " looked scared of the 🎃, so I switched them."

"And you knocked over the 📦 of 💸 by accident!" said 👱.

"Oops!" said Amy. "I just wanted you to have happy 🎃."

👦 laughed. "Like, that makes me happy! We thought the 🏠 was haunted."

🐕 barked. "Scooby-Dooby Doo!"

Did you spot all the picture clues in this Scooby-Doo mystery?

Each picture clue is on a flash card. Ask a grown-up to cut out the flash cards. Then try reading the words on the back of the cards. The pictures will be your clue.

Reading is fun with Scooby-Doo!

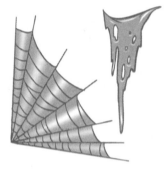

Scooby

house

webs

windows

pumpkins

tape

ghost	Daphne
Fred	Velma
Shaggy	tickets

door	box
Scooby Snacks	table
tree	floor

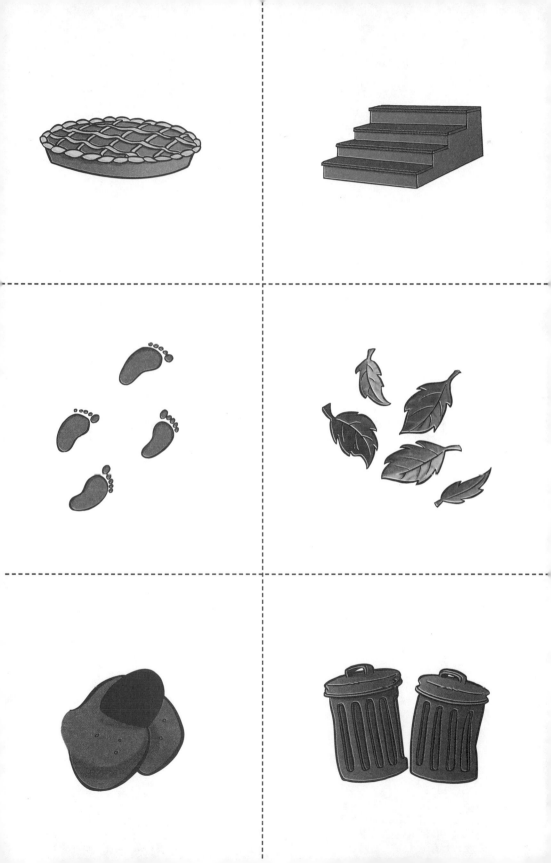

stairs	pie
leaves	footprints
trash cans	nose